The Joy of CHRISTMAS

Favorite Stories, Poems, and Recipes

illustrated by Kathy Mitchell

little rainbow®
Troll

Printed in Canada.

10 9 8 7 6 5 4 3 2

Library of Congress Cataloging-in-Publication Data
The joy of Christmas: favorite stories, poems, and recipes / illustrated by Kathy Mitchell.
p.   cm.
Summary: A collection of stories and poems about Christmas, including "The Christmas Spider," "Stocking Song on Christmas Eve," and "The Friendly Beasts."
ISBN 0-8167-3902-1 (lib.)   ISBN 0-8167-3783-5 (pbk.)
1. Christmas—Literary collections.   [1. Christmas—Literary collections.   2. Short stories.   3. Poetry—Collections.]
I. Mitchell, Kathy, ill.
PZ5.J8837   1995   808.8'033—dc20   95-19113

Contents

The Birth of Jesus

Luke 2:1, 3–18, 21

In those days Caesar Augustus published a decree ordering a census of the whole world. Everyone went to register, each to his own town. And so Joseph went from the town of Nazareth in Galilee to Judea, to David's town of Bethlehem— because he was of the house and lineage of David—to register with Mary, his espoused wife, who was with child.

While they were there, the days of her confinement were completed. She gave birth to her firstborn son and wrapped him in swaddling clothes and laid him in a manger, because there was no room for them in the place where travelers lodged.

There were shepherds in the region, living in the fields and keeping night watch by turns over their flocks. The angel of the Lord appeared to them as the glory of the Lord shown around them, and they were very much afraid. The angel said to them: "You have nothing to fear! I come to proclaim good news to you—tidings of great joy to be shared by the whole people. This day in David's city a savior has been born to you, the Messiah and Lord. Let this be a sign to you: In a manger you will find an infant wrapped in swaddling clothes." Suddenly there was with the angel a multitude of the heavenly host, praising God and saying, "Glory to God in high heaven, peace on Earth to those on whom his favor rests."

When the angels had returned to heaven, the shepherds said to one another: "Let us go over to Bethlehem and see this event which the Lord has made known to us." They went in haste and found Mary and Joseph, and the baby lying in the manger; once they saw, they understood what had been told them concerning this child. All who heard of it were astonished at the report given them by the shepherds.

When the eighth day arrived for his circumcision, the name Jesus was given the child, the name the angel had given him before he was conceived.

Now Christmas Is Come

Washington Irving

Now Christmas is come
Let's beat up the drum,
And call all our neighbors together,
And when they appear,
Let's make them such cheer
As will keep out the wind and the weather.

A Christmas Dream and How It Came True

Louisa May Alcott

"I'm so tired of Christmas I wish there would never be another one!" exclaimed a discontented-looking little girl as she sat idly watching her mother arrange a pile of gifts two days before they were to be given.

"Why, Effie, what a dreadful thing to say! You are as bad as old Scrooge; and I'm afraid something will happen to you, as it did to him, if you don't care for dear Christmas," answered Mamma, almost dropping the silver horn she was filling with delicious candies.

"Who was Scrooge? What happened to him?" asked Effie with a glimmer of interest in her listless face as she picked out the sourest lemon-drop she could find, for nothing sweet suited her just then.

"He was one of Dickens's best people, and you can read the charming story some day. He hated Christmas until a strange dream showed him how dear and beautiful it was, and made a better man of him."

"I shall read it; for I like dreams, and have a great many curious ones myself. But they don't keep me from being tired of Christmas," said Effie, poking discontentedly among the sweeties for something worth eating.

"Why are you tired of what should be the happiest time of all the year?" asked Mamma anxiously.

"Perhaps I shouldn't be if I had something new. But it is always the same, and there isn't any more surprise about it. I always find heaps of goodies in my stocking. Don't like some of them, and soon get tired of those I do like. We always have a great dinner, and I eat too much, and feel ill next day. Then there is a Christmas tree somewhere, with a doll on top, or a stupid old Santa Claus, and children dancing and screaming over bonbons and toys that break, and shiny things that are of no use. Really, Mamma, I've had so many Christmases all alike that I don't think I can bear another one." And Effie laid herself flat on the sofa, as if the mere idea was too much for her.

Her mother laughed at her despair but was sorry to see her little girl so discontented when she had everything to make her happy, and had known but ten Christmas days.

"Suppose we don't give you any presents at all—how would that suit you?" asked Mamma, anxious to please her spoiled child.

"I should like one large and splendid one, and one dear little one, to remember some very nice person by," said Effie, who was a fanciful little body, full of odd whims and notions, which her friends loved to gratify, regardless of time, trouble, or money; for she was the last of three little girls, and very dear to all the family.

"Well, my darling, I will see what I can do to please you, and not say a word until all is ready. If I could only get a new idea to start with!" And Mamma went on tying up her pretty bundles with a thoughtful face, while Effie strolled to the window to watch the rain that kept her indoors and made her dismal.

"Seems to me poor children have better times than rich ones. I can't go out, and there is a girl about my age splashing along, without any maid to fuss about rubbers and cloaks and umbrellas and colds. I wish I was a beggar-girl."

"Would you like to be hungry, cold, and ragged, to beg all day, and sleep on an ash heap at night?" asked Mamma, wondering what would come next.

"Cinderella did, and had a nice time in the end. This girl out here has a basket of scraps on her arm, and a big old shawl all around her, and doesn't seem to care a bit, though the water runs out of the toes of her boots. She goes paddling along, laughing at the rain, and eating a cold potato as if it tasted nicer than the chicken and ice cream I had for dinner. Yes, I do think poor children are happier than rich ones."

"So do I, sometimes. At the Orphan Asylum today I saw two dozen merry little souls who have no parents, no home, and no hope of Christmas beyond a stick of candy or cake. I wish you had been there to see how happy they were, playing with the old toys some richer children had sent them."

"You may give them all mine; I'm so tired of them I never want to see them again," said Effie, turning from the window to the pretty dollhouse full of everything a child's heart could desire.

"I will, and let you begin again with something you will not tire of, if I can only find it." And Mamma knit her brows trying to discover some grand surprise for this child who didn't care for Christmas.

Nothing more was said then; and wandering off to the library, Effie found *A Christmas Carol,* and curling herself up in the sofa corner, read it all before tea. Some of it she did not understand, but she laughed and cried over many parts of the charming story, and felt better without knowing why.

All the evening she thought of poor Tiny Tim, Mrs. Cratchit with the pudding, and the stout old gentleman who danced go gayly that "his legs twinkled in the air." Presently bedtime arrived.

"Come now, and toast your feet," said Effie's nurse, "while I do your pretty hair and tell stories."

"I'll have a fairy tale tonight, a very interesting one," commanded Effie as she put on her blue silk wrapper and little fur-lined slippers to sit before the fire and have her long curls brushed.

So Nursey told her best tales; and when at last the child lay down under her lace curtains, her head was full of a curious jumble of Christmas elves, poor children, snowstorms, sugarplums, and surprises. So it is no wonder that she dreamed all night; and this was the dream, which she never quite forgot.

She found herself sitting on a stone, in the middle of a great field, all alone. The snow was falling fast, a bitter wind whistled by, and night was coming on. She felt hungry, cold, and tired, and did not know where to go nor what to do.

"I wanted to be a beggar-girl, and now I am one; but I don't like it, and wish somebody would come and take care of me. I don't know who I am, and I think I must be lost," thought Effie with the curious interest one takes in oneself in dreams.

But the more she thought about it, the more bewildered she felt. Faster fell the snow, colder blew the wind, darker grew the night; and poor Effie made up her mind that she was quite forgotten and left to freeze alone. The tears were chilled on her cheeks, her feet felt like icicles, and her heart died within her, so hungry, frightened, and forlorn was she. Laying her head on her knees, she gave herself up for lost, and sat there with the great flakes turning her to a little white mound, when suddenly the sound of music reached her, and starting up, she looked and listened with all her eyes and ears.

Far away a dim light shone, and a voice was heard singing. She tried to run toward the welcome glimmer, but could not stir, and stood like a small statue of expectation while the light drew nearer, and the sweet words of the song grew clearer.

> "From our happy home
> Through the world we roam
> One week in all the year,

Making winter spring
With the joy we bring
For Christmastide is here.

"Now the eastern star
Shines from afar
To light the poorest home;
Hearts warmer grow
Gifts freely flow
For Christmastide has come.

"Now gay trees rise
Before young eyes,
Abloom with tempting cheer;
Blithe voices sing,
And blithe bells ring,
For Christmastide is here.

"Oh, happy chime,
Oh, blessed time,
That draws us all so near!
'Welcome, dear day,'
All creatures say,
For Christmastide is here."

A child's voice sang, a child's hand carried the

little candle; and in the circle of soft light it shed, Effie saw a pretty child coming to her through the night and snow. A rosy, smiling creature, wrapped in white fur, with a wreath of green and scarlet holly on its shining hair, the magic candle in one hand, and the other outstretched as if to shower gifts and warmly press all other hands.

Effie forgot to speak as this bright vision came nearer, leaving no trace of footsteps in the snow, only lighting the way with its little candle, and filling the air with the music of its song.

"Dear child, you are lost, and I have come to find you," said the stranger, taking Effie's cold hand in his, with a smile like sunshine, while every holly berry glowed like a little fire.

"Do you know me?" asked Effie, feeling no fear but a great gladness at his coming.

"I know all children, and I go to find them; for this is my holiday, and I gather them from all parts of the world to be merry with me once a year."

"Are you an angel?" asked Effie, looking for the wings.

"No; I am a Christmas spirit, and live with my friends in a pleasant place, getting ready for our holiday, when we are let out to roam about the world, helping to make this a happy time for all who will let us in. Will you come and see how we work?"

"I will go anywhere with you. Don't leave me again," cried Effie gladly.

"First I will make you comfortable. That is what we love to do. You are cold, and you shall be warm; hungry, and I will feed you; sorrowful, and I will make you gay."

With a wave of his candle all three miracles were wrought—for the snowflakes turned to a white fur coat and hood on Effie's head and shoulders; a bowl of hot soup came sailing to her lips, and vanished when she had eagerly drunk the last drop; and suddenly the dismal field changed to a new world so full of wonders that all her troubles were forgotten in a minute.

Bells were ringing so merrily that it was hard to keep from dancing. Green garlands hung on the walls, and every tree was a Christmas tree full of toys, and blazing with candles that never went out.

In one place many little spirits sewed like mad on warm clothes, turning off work faster than any sewing machine ever invented, and great piles were made ready to be sent to poor people. Other busy creatures packed money into purses, and wrote checks which they sent flying away on the wind— a lovely kind of snowstorm to fall into a world below full of poverty.

Older and graver spirits were looking over piles of little books, in which the records of the past year were kept, telling how different people had spent it, and what sort of gifts they deserved. Some got peace, some disappointment, some remorse and sorrow, some great joy and hope. The rich had generous thoughts sent them; the poor, gratitude and contentment. Children had more love and duty to parents; and parents renewed patience, wisdom, and satisfaction for and in their children. No one was forgotten.

"Please tell me what splendid place this is?" asked Effie as soon as she could collect her wits after the first look at all these astonishing things.

"This is the Christmas world; and here we work all the year round, never tired of getting ready for the happy day. See, these are the saints just setting off, for some have far to go, and the children must not be disappointed."

As he spoke the spirit pointed to four gates, out of which four great sleighs were just driving, laden with toys, while a jolly old Santa Claus sat in the middle of each, drawing on his mittens and tucking up his wraps for a long cold drive.

"Why, I thought there was only one Santa Claus, and even he was a humbug," cried Effie, astonished at the sight.

"Never give up your faith in the sweet old stories, even after you come to see that they are only the pleasant shadow of a lovely truth."

Just then the sleighs went off with a great jingling of bells and pattering of reindeer hoofs. All the spirits gave a cheer that was heard in the lower world, where people said, "Hear the stars sing."

"I never will say there isn't any Santa Claus again. Now, show me more."

"You will like to see this place, I think, and may learn something here perhaps."

The spirit smiled as he led the way to a little door, through which Effie peeped into a world of dolls. Dollhouses were in full blast, with dolls of all sorts going on like live people. Waxed ladies sat in their parlors elegantly dressed; some dolls cooked in the kitchens; nurses walked out with the bits of dollies; and the streets were full of tin soldiers marching, wooden horses prancing, express wagons rumbling; and little men hurrying to and fro. Shops were there, and tiny people buying legs of mutton, pounds of tea, mites of clothes, and everything dolls use or wear or want.

But presently she saw that in some ways the dolls improved upon the manners and customs of human beings, and she watched eagerly to learn why they did these things. A fine Paris doll driving in her carriage took up another doll who was hobbling along with a basket of clean clothes, and carried her to her journey's end, as if it were the proper thing to do. Another interesting china lady took off her comfortable red cloak and put it around a poor wooden creature done up in a paper shift, and so badly painted that its face would have sent some babies into fits.

"Seems to me I once knew a rich girl who didn't give her things to poor girls. I wish I could remember who she was, and tell her to be as kind as that china doll," said Effie, much touched at the sweet way the pretty creature wrapped up the poor fright, and then ran off in her little gray gown to buy a shiny fowl stuck on a wooden platter for her invalid mother's dinner.

"We recall these things to people's minds by dreams. I think the girl you speak of won't forget this one." And the spirit smiled, as if he enjoyed some joke which she did not see.

A little bell rang as she looked, and away scampered the children into the red-and-green schoolhouse with the roof that lifted up, so one could see how nicely they sat at their desks with mites of books, or drew on the inch-square blackboards with crumbs of chalk.

"They know their lessons very well, and are as

still as mice. We make a great racket at our school, and get bad marks every day. I shall tell the girls they had better mind what they do, or their dolls will be better scholars than they are," said Effie, much impressed, as she peeped in and saw no rod in the hand of the little mistress, who looked up and shook her head at the intruder, as if begging her to go away before the order of the school was disturbed.

Effie retired at once, but could not resist one look in the window of a fine mansion where the family was at dinner; the children behaved so well at the table, and never grumbled a bit when their mamma said they could not have any more fruit.

"Now show me something else," she said as they came again to the low door that led out of Doll land.

"You have seen how we prepare for Christmas; let me show you where we love best to send our good and happy gifts," answered the spirit, giving her his hand again.

"I know. I've seen ever so many," began Effie, thinking of her own Christmases.

"No, you have never seen what I will show you. Come away, and remember what you see tonight."

Like a flash that bright world vanished, and

Effie found herself in a part of the city she had never seen before. It was far away from the gayer places, where every store was brilliant with lights and full of pretty things, and every house wore a festival air, while people hurried to and fro with merry greetings. It was down among the dingy streets where the poor lived, and where there was no making ready for Christmas.

Hungry women looked in at the shabby shops, longing to buy meat and bread, but empty pockets forbade. Tipsy men drank up their wages in the barrooms; and in many cold dark chambers little children huddled under thick blankets, trying to forget their misery in sleep.

No nice dinners filled the air with savory smells, no gay trees dropped toys and bonbons into eager hands, no little stockings hung in rows beside the chimneypiece ready to be filled, no happy sounds of music, gay voices, and dancing feet were heard; and there were no signs of Christmas anywhere.

"Don't they have any in this place?" asked Effie, shivering, as she held fast the spirit's hand, following where he led her.

"We come to bring it. Let me show you our best workers." And the spirit pointed to some sweet-faced men and women who came stealing into the poor houses, working such beautiful miracles that Effie could only stand and watch.

Some slipped money into the empty pockets, and sent happy mothers to buy all the comforts they needed; others led the drunken men out of temptation, and took them home to find safer pleasures there. Fires were kindled on cold hearths, tables spread as if by magic, and warm clothes wrapped around shivering limbs. Flowers suddenly bloomed in the chambers of the sick; old people found themselves remembered; sad hearts were consoled by a tender word, and wicked ones softened by the story of Him who forgave all sin.

But the sweetest work was for the children. Effie held her breath to watch these human fairies hang up and fill the little stockings without which a child's Christmas is not perfect, putting in things that once she would have thought very humble presents, but which now seemed beautiful and precious because these poor babies had nothing.

"That is so beautiful! I wish I could make merry Christmas as these good people do, and be loved and thanked as they are," said Effie, softly, as she watched the busy men and women do their work and steal away without thinking of any reward but their own satisfaction.

"You can if you will. I have shown you the way.

Try it, and see how happy your own holiday will be hereafter."

As he spoke, the spirit seemed to put his arms around her, and vanished with a kiss.

"Oh, stay and show me more!" cried Effie, trying to hold him fast.

"Darling, wake up, and tell me why you are smiling in your sleep," said a voice in her ear; and opening her eyes, there was Mamma bending over her, and morning sunshine streaming into the room.

"Are they all gone? Did you hear the bells? Wasn't it splendid?" she asked, rubbing her eyes and looking about her for the pretty child who was so real and sweet.

"You have been dreaming at a great rate—talking in your sleep, laughing, and clapping your hands as if you were cheering someone. Tell me what was so splendid," said Mamma, soothing the tumbled hair and lifting up the sleepy head.

Then, while she was being dressed, Effie told her dream, and Nursey thought it very wonderful; but Mamma smiled to see how curiously things the child had thought, read, heard, and seen through the day were mixed up in her sleep.

"The spirit said I could work lovely miracles if I tried; but I don't know how to begin, for I have no magic candle to make feasts appear and light up groves of Christmas trees, as he did," said Effie sorrowfully.

"Yes you have. We will do it! We will do it!" And clapping her hands, Mamma began to dance all over the room as if she had lost her wits.

"How? How? You must tell me, Mamma," cried Effie, dancing after her, and ready to believe anything possible when she remembered the adventures of the past night.

"I've got it! I've got it!—the new idea. A splendid one, if I can only carry it out!" And Mamma waltzed the little girl around till her curls flew wildly in the air, while Nursey laughed as if she would die.

"Tell me! Tell me!" shrieked Effie.

"No, no; it's a surprise—a grand surprise for Christmas day!" sung Mamma, evidently charmed with her happy thought. "Now, come to breakfast, for we must work like bees if we want to play spirits tomorrow. You and Nursey will go out shopping, and get heaps of things, while I arrange matters behind the scenes."

They were running downstairs as Mamma spoke, and Effie called out breathlessly—

"It won't be a surprise; for I know you are going to ask some poor children here, and have a tree or something. It won't be like my dream; for they had ever so many trees, and more children than we can find anywhere."

"There will be no tree, no party, no dinner in this house at all, and no presents for you. Won't that be a surprise?" And Mamma laughed at Effie's bewildered face.

"Do it. I shall like it, I think; and I won't ask any questions, so it will all burst upon me when the time comes," she said; and she ate her breakfast thoughtfully, for this really would be a new sort of Christmas.

All that morning Effie trotted after Nursey in and out of shops, buying dozens of barking dogs, wooly lambs, and squeaking birds; tiny tea sets, gay picture books, mittens and hoods, dolls and candy. Parcel after parcel was sent home; but when Effie returned she saw no trace of them, though she peeped everywhere. Nursey chuckled, but wouldn't give a hint, and went out again in the afternoon with a long list of more things to buy while Effie wandered forlornly about the house, missing the usual merry stir that went before the Christmas dinner and the evening fun.

As for Mamma, she was quite invisible all day, and came in at night so tired that she could only lie on the sofa to rest, smiling as if some very pleasant thought made her happy in spite of weariness.

"Is the surprise going on all right?" asked Effie anxiously, for it seemed an immense time to wait till another evening came.

"Beautifully! Better than I expected; for several of my good friends are helping, or I couldn't have done as I wish. I know you will like it, dear, and long remember this new way of making Christmas merry."

Mamma gave her a very tender kiss, and Effie went to bed.

The next day was a very strange one; for when she woke there was no stocking to examine, no pile of gifts under her napkin, no one said, "Merry Christmas!" to her, and the dinner was just as usual to her. Mamma vanished again, and Nursey kept wiping her eyes and saying: "The dear things! It's the prettiest idea I ever heard of. No one but your blessed ma could have done it."

"Do stop, Nursey, or I shall go crazy because I don't know the secret!" cried Effie more than once; and she kept her eye on the clock, for at seven in the evening the surprise was to come off.

The longed-for hour arrived at last, and the child was too excited to ask questions when Nursey put on her cloak and hood, led her to the carriage, and they drove away, leaving their house the one dark and silent one in the row.

"I feel like the girls in the fairy tales who are led off to strange places and see fine things," said Effie, in a whisper, as they jingled through the gay streets.

"Ah, my deary, it *is* like a fairy tale, I do assure you, and you will see finer things than most children will tonight. Steady, now, and do just as I tell you, and don't say one word whatever you see," answered Nursey, quite quivering with excitement as she patted a large box in her lap, and nodded and laughed with twinkling eyes.

They drove into a dark yard, and Effie was led through a back door to a little room, where Nursey coolly proceeded to take off not only Effie's cloak and hood but her dress and shoes also. Effie stared and bit her lips, but kept still until out of the box came a little white fur coat and boots, a wreath of holly leaves and berries, and a candle with a frill of gold paper around it. A long "Oh!" escaped her then; and when she was dressed and saw herself in the glass, she started back, exclaiming, "Why, Nursey, I look like the spirit in my dream!"

"So you do; and that's the part you are to play, my pretty! Now whist, while I blind your eyes and put you in your place."

"Shall I be afraid?" whispered Effie, full of

wonder; for as they went out she heard the sound of many voices, the tramp of many feet, and, in spite of the bandage, was sure a great light shone upon her when she stopped.

"You needn't be; I shall stand close by, and your ma will be there."

After the handkerchief was tied about her eyes, Nursey led Effie up some steps, and placed her on a high platform where something like leaves touched her head, and the soft snap of lamps seemed to fill the air.

Music began as soon as Nursey clapped her hands, the voices outside sounded nearer, and the tramp was evidently coming up the stairs.

"Now, my precious, look and see how you and your dear ma have made a merry Christmas for them that needed it!"

Off went the bandage, and for a minute Effie really did think she was asleep again, for she actually stood in "a grove of Christmas trees," all gay and shining as in her vision. Twelve on a side, in two rows down the room, stood the little pines, each on its low table and behind Effie a taller one rose to the roof, hung with wreaths of popcorn, apples, oranges, horns of candy, and cakes of all sorts, from sugary hearts to gingerbread Jumbos. On the smaller trees she saw many of her own discarded toys and those Nursey bought, as well as heaps that seemed to have rained down straight from that delightful Christmas country where she felt as if she was again.

"How splendid! Who is it for? What is that noise? Where is Mamma?" cried Effie, pale with pleasure and surprise as she stood looking down the brilliant little street from her high place.

Before Nursey could answer, the doors at the lower end flew open, and in marched twenty-four little blue-gowned orphan girls, singing sweetly, until amazement changed the song to cries of joy and wonder as the shining spectacle appeared. While they stood staring with round eyes at the wilderness of pretty things about them, Mamma stepped up beside Effie, and holding her hand fast to give her courage, told the story of the dream in a few simple words, ending in this way:

"So my little girl wanted to be a Christmas spirit too, and make this a happy day for those who had not as many pleasures and comforts as she has. She likes surprises, and we planned this for you all. She shall play the good fairy, and give each of you something from this tree, after which everyone will find her own name on a small tree, and can go to enjoy it in her own way. March by, my dears, and let us fill your hands."

Nobody told them to do it, but all the hands were clapped heartily before a single child stirred; then one by one they came to look up wonderingly at the pretty giver of the feast as she leaned down to offer them great yellow oranges, red apples, bunches of grapes, bonbons, and cakes, till all were gone, and a double row of smiling faces turned toward her as the children filed back to their places in the orderly way they had been taught.

Then each was led to her own tree by the good ladies who had helped Mamma with all their hearts; and the happy hubbub that arose would have satisfied even Santa Claus himself—shrieks of joy, dances of delight, laughter and tears (for some tender little things could not bear so much pleasure at once, and sobbed with mouths full of candy and hands full of toys). How they ran to show one another the new treasures! How they peeped and tasted, pulled and pinched, until the air was full of queer noises, the floor covered with papers, and the little trees left bare of all but candles!

"I don't think heaven can be any gooder than this," sighed one small girl as she looked about her in a blissful maze, holding her full apron with one hand while she luxuriously carried sugarplums to her mouth with the other.

"Is that a truly angel up there?" asked another, fascinated by the little white figure with the wreath on its shining hair, who in some mysterious way had been the cause of all this merrymaking.

"I wish I dared to go and kiss her for this splendid party," said a lame child, leaning on her crutch as she stood near the steps, wondering how it seemed to sit in a mother's lap, as Effie was doing, while she watched the happy scene before her.

Effie heard her, and remembering Tiny Tim, ran down and put her arms about the pale child, kissing the wistful face as she said sweetly, "You may; but Mamma deserves the thanks. She did it all; I only dreamed about it."

Lame Katy felt as if "a truly angel" was embracing her, and could only stammer out her thanks, while the other children ran to see the pretty spirit and touch her soft dress, until she stood in a crowd of blue gowns laughing as they held up their gifts for her to see and admire.

Mamma leaned down and whispered one word to the older girls, and suddenly they all took hands to dance around Effie, singing as they skipped.

It was a pretty sight, and the ladies found it hard to break up the happy revel; but it was late for small people, and too much fun is a mistake.

So the girls fell into line, and marched before Effie and Mamma again, to say good night with such grateful little faces that the eyes of those who looked grew dim with tears. Mamma kissed every one; and many a hungry childish heart felt as if the touch of those tender lips was their best gift. Effie shook so many small hands that her own tingled; and when Katy came she pressed a small doll into Effie's hand, whispering, "You didn't have a single present, and we had lots. Do keep that; it's the prettiest thing I got."

"I will," answered Effie, and held it fast until the last smiling face was gone, the surprise all over, and she safe in her own bed, too tired and happy for anything but sleep.

"Mamma, it was a beautiful surprise, and I thank you so much! I don't see how you ever did it; but I like it best of all the Christmases I ever had, and I mean to make one every year. I had my splendid big present, and here is the dear little one to keep for love of poor Katy; so even that part of my wish came true."

And Effie fell asleep with a happy smile on her lips, her one humble gift still in her hand, and a new love for Christmas in her heart that never changed through a long life spent in doing good.

The Christmas Spider

A Polish Folktale

retold by Marguerite de Angeli

The gray spider worked very hard every day making long strands of silk that he wove into a web in which he caught troublesome flies. But he noticed that everyone turned away from him because, they said, he was so unpleasant to look at with his long, crooked legs and furry body. Of course the gray spider didn't believe that, because he had only the kindliest feelings for everybody. One day when he was crossing the stream he looked into the water. There he saw himself as he really was.

"Oh," he thought, "I am very unpleasant to look at. I shall keep out of people's way." He was very sad and hid himself in the darkest corner of the stable. There he again began to work as he always had, weaving long strands of silk into webs and catching flies. The donkey and the ox and the sheep who lived in the stable thanked him for his kindness, because they were no longer bothered with the buzzing flies. That made the spider very happy.

One night, exactly at midnight, the spider was awakened by a brilliant light. He looked about and saw that the light came from the manger where a tiny Child lay on the hay. The stable was filled with glory, and over the Child bent a beautiful mother. Behind her stood a man with a staff in his hand, and the ox and the donkey and all the white sheep were down on their knees.

Suddenly a gust of cold wind swept through the stable and the Baby began to weep from the cold. The mother bent over Him but could not cover Him enough to keep Him warm. The little spider took his silken web and laid it at Mary's feet (for it was Mary), and Mary took up the web and covered the Baby with it. It was soft as thistledown and as warm as wool. The Child stopped His crying and smiled at the little gray spider.

Then Mary said, "Little gray spider, for this great gift to the Babe you may have anything you wish."

"Most of all," said the spider, "I wish to be beautiful."

"That I cannot give you," Mary answered. "You must stay as you are for as long as you live. But this I grant you. Whenever anyone sees a spider at evening, he will count it as a good omen, and it shall bring him good fortune."

This made the spider very happy, and to this day, on Christmas Eve, we cover the Christmas tree with "angel's hair" in memory of the gray spider and his silken web.

Stocking Song on Christmas Eve

Mary Mapes Dodge

Welcome Christmas! heel and toe,
Here we wait thee in a row.
Come, good Santa Claus, we beg,
Fill us tightly, foot and leg.

Fill us quickly ere you go,—
Fill us till we overflow,
That's the way! and leave us more
Heaped in piles upon the floor.

Little feet that ran all day
Twitch in dreams of merry play,
Little feet that jumped at will
Lie all pink and white and still.

See us, how we lightly swing,
Hear us, how we try to sing,
Welcome Christmas! heel and toe,
Come and fill us ere you go!

Here we hang till someone nimbly
Jumps with treasures down the chimney.
Bless us! how he'll tickle us!
Funny old Saint Nicholas.

A Present for Santa Claus

Carolyn Haywood

There were many signs that Christmas would soon be here. At night the main street looked like fairyland. Tiny electric lights were strung all over the branches of the bare trees. The children talked of Santa Claus and when they would go to see him.

One Saturday morning when Star came into the kitchen for her breakfast, she said to her mother, "Today's the day, isn't it? I'm going to see Santa Claus!"

"That's right," her mother replied.

"When will we go?" Star asked as she sat down to eat her bowl of oatmeal.

"We'll go as soon as I finish clearing up the kitchen," her mother replied.

As soon as Star finished her breakfast, she said, "I'll put my things on and feed the turtles." Star had two turtles that she had named Mable and Marble.

Star went into her room. She kept her turtles in a glass tank. She picked up a box of turtle food and sprinkled it around the turtles. Then she scratched their backs and said, "Now eat your breakfast. I'm going to see Santa Claus."

When Star and her mother were ready to leave, Star was wearing her blue snow pants and her warm red jacket and cap. Just as her mother opened the door Star cried out, "Oh, Mommy! I haven't any present for Santa Claus."

"You don't take presents to Santa Claus, Star," her mother said. "Santa Claus brings presents to you."

"Oh, but I want a present for him," said Star.

"Now, Star!" said her mother. "Nobody takes presents to Santa Claus."

"But it's Christmas," said Star. "Everybody takes everybody a present."

"Everybody does not take everybody a present," said her mother. "Now come along."

Star shook her head. "Everybody should take Santa Claus a present, because he gives presents to everybody's children. I have to take him a present. Maybe he's like me. Maybe it's his birthday."

Star's mother sat down on the chair beside the door. She held her head and said, "Darling! It is not Santa Claus's birthday. You don't have a present for him, you don't need a present for him, and he doesn't want a present."

"Everybody wants presents, Mommy," said Star, almost in tears. "I'll go find something." She darted up the stairs.

She wasn't gone long. When she came down she had a satisfied look on her face. "I'm going to give Mabel to Santa Claus," she said.

"Mabel!" her mother exclaimed. "What will Santa Claus do with Mabel?"

"He'll love Mabel," Star replied.

Star's mother shook her head. "Come along," she said, opening the door. She took Star's hand and hurried her to the bus stop.

When they were seated in the bus, her mother said, "Where is Mabel?"

"In my pocket," Star replied. "In the pocket of my snow pants."

"I hope Mabel's happy in your pocket," her mother said. "It doesn't seem to be the best place for a little turtle."

"She's all right," said Star. "I put my hand in and tickle her every once in awhile. Mabel likes being tickled."

"You're sure you want to give her away?" her mother asked. "You've been very fond of your turtles."

"Well, I didn't have time to find anything else for a present for Santa Claus," said Star, "so I went over to Mabel and I said, 'Mabel, you're going to be a present for Santa Claus.' Then I said, 'I guess you don't know about Santa Claus, but he's not a turtle.' "

Star looked up at her mother. "I wanted Mabel to know that he isn't a turtle, so she won't be surprised when she sees him. I told her he's a sort of magic person. And you know something, Mommy?"

"What?" her mother asked.

"Well, once in a fairy story a frog got turned into a handsome prince, so maybe Santa Claus can turn Mabel into a beautiful princess." Star turned and gazed out the window. "She'd be Princess Mabel!" she said with a sigh.

Star's mother sighed, too. Then she said, "I don't believe turning turtles into princesses is exactly Santa Claus's line. He's very busy in the toy business."

Star poked her finger into her pocket and tickled Mabel. "Well, I think I'll call her Princess Mabel anyway."

When Star and her mother reached the store, they went directly to the toy department, where they found Santa Claus. Star stood holding her mother's hand and stared at Santa Claus. There he sat in a big red chair on a platform. He looked magnificent in his bright red suit trimmed with white fur and his shiny black boots. He held a little boy on his knee. Star saw the boy whisper into Santa Claus's ear, and she saw Santa Claus's white teeth when he laughed and put the little boy down.

There were several children standing in a line waiting to speak to Santa Claus. Star's mother took her to the end of the line and said, "You wait here until it's your turn to speak to Santa Claus."

"You'll wait with me, won't you, Mommy?"

"I'll stand nearby," her mother replied.

"Where shall I put my present for Santa Claus?" Star asked. "He doesn't have any Christmas tree."

"Well, you certainly couldn't hang Mabel on a Christmas tree, even if he had one," said her mother. "You see, Star, none of these children have presents for Santa Claus."

"That's because they forgot," said Star as she moved forward in the line.

Star watched as the children ahead of her reached Santa Claus. Some he took on his lap and some stood by his knee. When the little boy ahead of her began to talk to Santa Claus, Star put her hand into her pocket. She was surprised, for she couldn't find Mabel. She thought perhaps she had forgotten which pocket she had put her in, so she dug into her other one. Mabel was not there.

Now the little boy had gone, and Santa Claus was beckoning to Star. She was still poking around in her pocket when she reached his knee.

"Hello!" said Santa Claus in his big, cheery voice. "What's your name?"

"I'm Star," she replied, just as her finger went through a hole in her pocket.

Santa Claus leaned over and said, "What seems to be the matter?"

"I brought you a present," Star replied, "but I can't find it." Star dug down and made the hole in her pocket bigger.

"What is it you're trying to find?" Santa Claus asked.

"Mabel!" Star replied.

"Oh!" said Santa Claus.

"I guess she fell through the hole in my pocket," said Star, leaning over like a jackknife. Then she unzipped the bottom of the leg of her snow pants. She straightened up and said, "I'll shake my leg, and maybe she'll fall out."

"That's the thing!" said Santa Claus. "Shake a leg!"

Star shook and then she jumped while everyone stood around and watched her. Mabel did not appear. "I'll find her," said Star. "She's hiding!"

Star sat down on the floor beside Santa Claus's big black boots. She felt inside the leg of her pants and suddenly her face broke into a wide smile. "I found her!" she said, looking up at Santa Claus.

"Good!" said Santa Claus. "I can't wait to see Mabel."

Star leaned against Santa Claus's knee. "Hold out your hand," she said. Santa Claus held out his big hand, and Star placed the tiny turtle on her back in his palm. "I hope she's all right," said Star. "If she kicks her legs, she's alive."

Santa Claus's great big head in his red cap bent over his hand as Star leaned against him. Their heads were together as they watched to see if Mabel would kick her legs. Suddenly Star cried out, "She's alive! Mabel's alive!"

"Sure enough!" said Santa Claus. "She's alive and kicking!"

Star looked up into Santa Claus's face. "I'm sorry I couldn't wrap up your present," she said. "You don't mind if Mabel isn't wrapped, do you?"

Santa Claus drew Star to him and gave her a great big hug. "I never had a nicer present than Mabel," he said. "Thank you, and a merry Christmas to you."

As she walked away Star turned and looked back at Santa Claus. He waved his hand. Star waved, too, and called back, "Mabel likes hamburger! Just a teenie-weenie bit, of course."

"I'll remember," Santa Claus promised. "Hamburger for her Christmas dinner!"

On Christmas morning, when Star went to the fireplace in the living room, standing on the hearth was a beautiful doll dressed like a princess with a crown on her head. A card stood beside her. It said: *This is Princess Mabel, from Santa Claus.*

The Legend of the Candy Cane

Of all the beautiful traditions of Christmas, few are so ancient in meaning and so rich in symbolism as the simple candy cane.

It's shape is the crook of the Shepherd
One of the first who came;

The lively peppermint flavor is the regal gift of spice
The white is Jesus' purity, the red his sacrifice;

The narrow stripes are friendship and the nearness
of his love
Eternal sweet compassion, a gift from God above;

The candy cane reminds us all of just how much
God cared
And like his Christmas gift to us, it's meant to be
broken and shared.

Yes, Virginia, There Is a Santa Claus

In 1897, a young girl named Virginia O'Hanlon lived in New York City. She wrote this letter to the *New York Sun.*

> Dear Editor:
>   I am eight years old. Some of my little friends say that there is no Santa Claus. Papa says, "If you see it in the *Sun,* it's so." Please tell me the truth. Is there a Santa Claus?
>
> Virginia O'Hanlon

An editor named Francis P. Church responded to Virginia's letter in this editorial.

Is There a Santa Claus?

Virginia, your little friends are wrong. They have been affected by the skepticism of a skeptical age. They think that nothing can be which is not comprehensible by their little minds. They do not believe except what they see.

Yes, Virginia, there is a Santa Claus. He exists as certainly as love and generosity and devotion exist. Alas, how dreary the world would be if there were no Santa Claus! It would be as dreary as if there were no Virginias! There would be no childlike faith, then, no poetry, no romance, to make tolerable this existence.

You might get your papa to hire men to watch all the chimneys on Christmas Eve to catch Santa Claus; but even if they did not see Santa Claus coming down, what would that prove? Not everybody sees Santa Claus. The most real things in the world are those that neither children nor men see.

No Santa Claus! Thank God, he lives, and he lives forever. A thousand years from now, Virginia, nay, ten times ten thousand years from now, he will continue to make glad the heart of childhood.

little tree

e. e. cummings

little tree
little silent Christmas tree
you are so little
you are more like a flower

who found you in the green forest
and were you very sorry to come away?
see   i will comfort you
because you smell so sweetly

i will kiss your cool bark
and hug you safe and tight
just as your mother would,
only don't be afraid

look   the spangles
that sleep all the year in a dark box
dreaming of being taken out and allowed to shine,
the balls the chains red and gold the fluffy threads,

put up your little arms
and i'll give them all to you to hold
every finger shall have its ring
and there won't be a single place dark or unhappy

that when you're quite dressed
you'll stand in the window for everyone to see
and how they'll stare!
oh but you'll be very proud

and my little sister and i will take hands
and looking up at our beautiful tree
we'll dance and sing
"Noel Noel"

Christmas at Mole End

Kenneth Grahame

from THE WIND IN THE WILLOWS

*Rat and Mole are on their way to Rat's house at River Bank.
Along the way, they stop at Mole's house.*

"What a capital little house this is!" Mr. Rat
called out cheerily. "So compact! So well planned!
Everything here and everything in its place! We'll
make a jolly night of it. The first thing we want is
a good fire; I'll see to that—I always know where to
find things. So this is the parlor? Splendid! Your
own idea, those little sleeping bunks in the wall?
Capital! Now, I'll fetch the wood and the coals, and
you get a duster, Mole—you'll find one in the
drawer of the kitchen—and try and smarten things
up a bit. Bustle about, old chap!"

Encouraged by his inspiriting companion, the
Mole roused himself and dusted and polished with
energy and heartiness, while Rat, running to and
fro with armfuls of fuel, soon had a cheerful blaze
roaring up the chimney. He hailed the Mole to come
and warm himself; but Mole promptly had another

fit of the blues, dropping down on a couch in dark despair and burying his face in his duster.

"Rat," he moaned, "how about your supper, you poor, cold, hungry, weary animal? I've nothing to give you—nothing—not a crumb!"

"What a fellow you are for giving in!" said the Rat reproachfully. "Why, only just now I saw a sardine opener on the kitchen dresser, quite distinctly; and everybody knows that means there are sardines about somewhere in the neighborhood. Rouse yourself! Pull yourself together, and come with me and forage."

They went and foraged accordingly, hunting through every cupboard and turning out every drawer. The result was not so very depressing after all, though of course it might have been better: a tin of sardines, a box of captain's biscuits, nearly full, and a German sausage encased in silver paper.

"There's a banquet for you!" observed the Rat as he arranged the table. "I know some animals who would give their ears to be sitting down to supper with us tonight!"

"No bread!" groaned the Mole dolorously; "no butter, no—"

"No *pâté de foie gras,* no champagne!" continued the Rat, grinning. "And that reminds me—what's the little door at the end of the passage? Your cellar, of course! Every luxury in this house! Just you wait a minute."

He made for the cellar door, and presently reappeared somewhat dusty, with a bottle of cider in each paw and another under each arm. "Self-indulgent beggar you seem to be, Mole," he observed. "Deny yourself nothing. This is really the jolliest little place I ever was in. Now, wherever did you pick up those prints? Make the place look so homelike, they do. No wonder you're so fond of it, Mole. Tell us about it, and how you came to make it what it is."

Then, while the Rat busied himself fetching plates, and knives and forks, and mustard which he mixed in an eggcup, the Mole, his bosom still heaving with the stress of his recent emotion, related—somewhat shyly at first, but with more freedom as he warmed to his subject—how this was planned, and how that was thought out, and how this was got through a windfall from an aunt, and that was a wonderful find and a bargain, and this other thing was bought out of laborious savings and a certain amount of "going without." His spirits finally quite restored, he must needs go and caress his possessions, and take a lamp and show off their points to his visitor, and expatiate on them, quite forgetful of the supper they both so much needed; Rat, who was desperately hungry but strove to conceal it, nodding seriously, examining with a puckered brow, and saying, "Wonderful," and "Most remarkable," at intervals, when the chance for an observation was given him.

At last the Rat succeeded in decoying him to the table, and had just got seriously to work with the sardine opener when sounds were heard from the forecourt without—sounds like the scuffling of small feet in the gravel and a confused murmur of tiny voices, while broken sentences reached them: "Now, all in a line—hold the lantern up a bit, Tommy—clear your throats first—no coughing after I say one, two, three, Where's young Bill?— Here, come on, do, we're all a-waiting—"

"What's up?" inquired the Rat, pausing in his labors.

"I think it must be the field mice," replied the Mole with a touch of pride in his manner. "They go around carol-singing regularly at this time of the year. They're quite an institution in these parts. And they never pass me over—they come to Mole End last of all; and I used to give them hot drinks, and supper too sometimes, when I could afford it. It will be like old times to hear them again."

"Let's have a look!" cried the Rat, jumping up and running to the door.

It was a pretty sight, and a seasonable one, that

met their eyes when they flung the door open. In the forecourt, lit by the dim rays of a horn lantern, some eight or ten little field mice stood in a semicircle, red worsted comforters around their throats, their forepaws thrust deep into their pockets, their feet jigging for warmth. With bright beady eyes they glanced shyly at each other, sniggering a little, sniffing and applying coatsleeves a good deal. As the door opened, one of the elder ones that carried the lantern was just saying, "Now then, one, two, three!" and forthwith their shrill little voices uprose on the air, singing one of the old-time carols that their forefathers composed in fields that were fallow and held by frost, or when snowbound in chimney corners, and handed down to be sung in the miry street to lamplit windows.

"Villagers all, this frosty tide,
Let your doors swing open wide,
Though wind may follow, and snow beside,
Yet draw us in by your fire to bide;
Joy shall be yours in the morning!

"Here we stand in the cold and the sleet,
Blowing fingers and stamping feet,
Come from far away you to greet—
You by the fire and we in the street—
Bidding you joy in the morning!

"For ere one half of the night was gone,
Sudden a star has led us on,
Raining bliss and benison—
Bliss tomorrow and more anon,
Joy for every morning!

"Goodman Joseph toiled through the snow—
Saw the star o'er a stable low;
Mary she might not further go—
Welcome thatch, and little below!
Joy was hers in the morning.

"And then they heard the angels tell
'Who were the first to cry Noel?
Animals all, as it befell,
In the stable where they did dwell!
Joy shall be theirs in the morning!' "

The voices ceased, the singers, bashful but smiling, exchanged sidelong glances, and silence succeeded—but for a moment only.

Then, from up above and far away, down the tunnel they had so lately traveled, was borne to their ears in a faint musical hum the sound of distant bells ringing a joyful and clangorous peal.

"Very well sung, boys!" cried the Rat heartily. "And now come along in, all of you, and warm yourselves by the fire, and have something hot!"

"Yes, come along, field mice," cried the Mole eagerly. "This is quite like old times! Shut the door after you. Pull up that settle to the fire. Now, you just wait a minute while we—O, Ratty!" he cried in despair, plumping down on a seat, with tears impending. "Whatever are we doing? We've nothing to give them!"

"You leave all that to me," said the masterful Rat. "Here, you with the lantern! Come over this way. I want to talk to you. Now, tell me, are there any shops open at this hour of the night?"

"Why, certainly, sir," replied the field mouse respectfully. "At this time of the year our shops keep open to all sorts of hours."

"Then look here!" said the Rat. "You go off at once, you and your lantern, and you get me . . ."

Here much muttered conversation ensued, and the Mole only heard bits of it, such as—"Fresh, mind!—no, a pound of that will do—see you get Buggins's, for I won't have any other—no, only the best—if you can't get it there, try somewhere else— yes, of course, homemade, no tinned stuff—well, then, do the best you can!" Finally, there was a chink of coin passing from paw to paw, the field mouse was provided with an ample basket for his purchases, and off he hurried, he and his lantern.

The rest of the field mice, perched in a row on the settle, their small legs swinging, gave themselves up to the enjoyment of the fire, and toasted their chilblains till they tingled; while the Mole, failing to draw them into easy conversation, plunged into family history and made each of them recite the names of his numerous brothers, who were too young, it appeared, to be allowed to go out a-caroling this year, but looked forward very shortly to winning the parental consent.

The Rat, meanwhile, was busy examining the label on one of the cider bottles. "I perceive this to be Old Burton," he remarked approvingly. "Sensible Mole! The very thing! Now we shall be able to heat up some cider! Get the things ready, Mole, while I draw the corks."

It did not take long to prepare the brew and thrust the tin heater well into the red heart of the fire; and soon every field mouse was forgetting he had ever been cold in all his life.

"They act plays too, these fellows," the Mole explained to the Rat. "Make them up all by themselves, and act them afterward. And very well they do it, too! They gave us a capital one last year, about a field mouse who was captured at sea by a Barbary corsair, and made to row in a galley; and when he escaped and got home again, his ladylove had gone into a convent. Here, you! You were in it, I remember. Get up and recite a bit."

The field mouse addressed got up on his legs, giggled shyly, looked around the room, and remained absolutely tongue-tied. His comrades cheered him on, Mole coaxed and encouraged him, and the Rat went so far as to take him by the shoulders and shake him; but nothing could overcome his stage fright. They were busily engaged on him like watermen applying the Royal Humane Society's regulations to a case of long submersion, when the latch clicked, the door opened, and the field mouse with the lantern reappeared, staggering under the weight of his basket.

There was no more talk of play-acting once the very real and solid contents of the basket had been tumbled out on the table. Under the generalship of Rat, everybody was set to do something or to fetch something. In a very few minutes supper was ready, and Mole, as he took the head of the table in a sort of dream, saw a lately barren board set thick with savory comforts; saw his little friends' faces brighten and beam as they fell to without delay; and then let himself loose—for he was famished indeed—on the provender so magically provided, thinking what a happy homecoming this had turned out, after all. As they ate, they talked of old times, and the field mice gave him the local gossip up to date, and answered as well as they could the hundred questions he had to ask them. The Rat said little or nothing, only taking care that each guest had what he wanted, and plenty of it, and that Mole had no trouble or anxiety about anything.

They clattered off at last, very grateful and showering wishes of the season, with their jacket pockets stuffed with remembrances for the small brothers and sisters at home. When the door had closed on the last of them and the chink of the lanterns had died away, Mole and Rat kicked the fire up, drew their chairs in, and discussed the events of the long day. At last the Rat, with a tremendous yawn, said, "Mole, old chap, I'm ready to drop. Sleep is simply not the word. That your own bunk over on that side? Very well, then, I'll take this. What a ripping little house this is! Everything so handy!"

He clambered into his bunk and rolled himself well up in the blankets, and slumber gathered him forthwith, as a swath of Barley is folded into the arms of the reaping machine.

The weary Mole also was glad to turn in without delay, and soon had his head on his pillow, in great joy and contentment. But ere he closed his eyes he let them wander round his old room, mellow in the glow of the firelight that played or rested on familiar and friendly things which had long been unconsciously a part of him, and now smilingly received him back, without rancor. He was now in just the frame of mind that the tactful Rat had quietly worked to bring about in him. He saw clearly how plain and simple—how narrow, even—it all was; but clearly, too, how much it all meant to him, and the special value of some such anchorage in one's existence. He did not at all want to abandon the new life and its splendid spaces, to turn his back on sun and air and all they offered him and creep home and stay there; the upper world was all too strong, it called to him still, even down there, and he knew he must return to the larger stage. But it was good to think he had this to come back to, this place which was all his own, these things which were so glad to see him again and could always be counted upon for the same simple welcome.

The Friendly Beasts

Old English Carol

Jesus, our brother, strong and good,
Was humbly born in a stable rude;
And the friendly beasts around Him stood,
Jesus, our brother, strong and good.

"I," said the sheep with curly horn.
"I gave Him my wool for His blanket warm.
"He wore my coat on Christmas morn,
"I," said the sheep with the curly horn.

"I," said the dove from rafters high.
"I cooed Him to sleep so He would not cry,
"We cooed Him to sleep, my mate and I;
"I," said the dove from rafters high.

"I," said the cow, all white and red.
"I gave Him my manger for His bed;
"I gave Him my hay to pillow His head;
"I," said the cow, all white and red.

"I," said the donkey, shaggy and brown.
"I carried His mother uphill and down;
"I carried her safely to Bethlehem town,
"I," said the donkey, shaggy and brown.

And every beast, by some good spell,
In the stable dark was glad to tell,
Of the gift he gave Emmanuel,
The gift he gave Emmanuel.

Santa Claus

Anonymous

He comes in the night! He comes in the night!
He softly, silently comes,
While the sweet little heads on the pillows so white
Are dreaming of bugles and drums.
He cuts through the snow like a ship through
    the foam,
While the white flakes 'round him whirl.
Who tells him I know not, but he finds the home
Of each good little boy and girl.

His sleigh is long, and deep, and wide.
It will carry a host of things,
While dozens of drums hang over the side,
With sticks sticking under the strings.
And yet not the sound of a drum is heard,
Not a bugle blast is blown,
As he mounts to the chimney-top like a bird,
And drops to the hearth like a stone.

The little red stockings he silently fills,
Till the stockings will hold no more.
The bright little sleds for the great snow hills
Are quickly set down on the floor.
Then Santa Claus mounts to the roof like a bird,
And glides to his seat in the sleigh.
Not the sound of a bugle or drum is heard
As he noiselessly gallops away.

Secrets

Anonymous

Secrets big and secrets small
On the eve of Christmas.
Such keen ears has every wall
That we whisper, one and all,
On the eve of Christmas.

Secrets upstairs, secrets down,
On the eve of Christmas.
Daddy brings them from the town,
Wrapped in papers stiff and brown
On the eve of Christmas.

But the secret best of all,
On the eve of Christmas,
Steals right down the chimney tall,
Fills our stockings, one and all,
On the eve of Christmas.

The Nutcracker

Anonymous

A long time ago, in a land not so very far away, lived a little girl named Marie. Marie loved to play games and dance and draw pretty pictures. But, most of all—more than anything else—Marie loved Christmas.

One year, on Christmas Eve, Marie's father and mother had a party. Everyone in the village was there. There was music and dancing and all sorts of games and magic tricks. A huge tree filled the room and glittered with sparkling lights and tinsel.

Beneath the tree, in all shapes and colors, were the presents. When the time came to open them, the children quickly tore away the bright paper. What treasures they found! There were shiny brass trumpets and big fuzzy bears; lovely china dolls and bright tin soldiers. It was truly a wonderful Christmas.

And yet, the most wonderful part was still to come. Marie had a godfather. His name was Herr

Drosselmeyer. Herr Drosselmeyer was a very unusual man. He wore a black patch over his right eye, and his long white hair stuck out wildly from his head. And Herr Drosselmeyer also had a very special skill—he was an excellent toymaker! This Christmas, Herr Drosselmeyer was bringing a special present just for Marie.

All the other gifts had already been opened. The guests were eating cakes and candies. The children were playing with their new toys.

When Herr Drosselmeyer suddenly appeared, the children were afraid—all except Marie. Happily, she ran to give him a hug. And then, he presented her with the best present of all.

"What did you get?"

The children crowded around as Marie quickly opened the small box.

"Ooooh," sighed Marie. "What a lovely little man."

The little man was a Nutcracker. He was dressed as a soldier. His mouth opened and closed. And his teeth were strong enough to crack the hardest of nuts.

"He looks so real," cried the children. It was true. The Nutcracker did look real. And yet, he was only made of wood.

Then something awful happened. Fritz, Marie's

brother, grabbed the Nutcracker and ran off. Marie took off after him. In the excitement, Fritz dropped the little man.

"Oh, no," cried Marie. "He's broken."

Sure enough, the little Nutcracker's jaw had snapped. Marie was heartbroken.

"Come now, my child," said Herr Drosselmeyer. "He'll be all right. See, I'll just wrap my handkerchief around his head to keep his mouth shut. Don't worry. He'll be as good as new in the morning."

With that, the old man scooped up the broken toy. He placed it in a tiny bed—just the right size for a Nutcracker. Marie sniffled a bit more, but she felt better. Somehow, she knew Herr Drosselmeyer was right.

As the hour grew late, the guests said good night. And one by one, they left. Marie went upstairs to bed. So did her parents and her brother Fritz. The house became quite still.

But Marie couldn't sleep. Silently, she tiptoed down the stairs to take another peek at her Nutcracker. Marie began to feel a bit uneasy. It was dark downstairs, and very quiet and still. The tree looked so big. And the toys looked so real. . . .

Just then the clock struck midnight. Quickly, Marie turned around. And there, perched on the top of the clock was an owl. And somehow, the owl looked very much like Herr Drosselmeyer.

Marie didn't have much time to wonder about this. All sorts of strange things were happening at once. The Christmas tree grew taller and taller. The room grew larger. And the toys, scattered about the tree, began to move. The soldiers and the dolls— and even the Nutcracker—were all coming to life!

Marie could hardly believe her eyes. But that wasn't all. She heard strange squeaks and creaks and rustling noises. Suddenly, an army of giant gray mice appeared. Now Marie was really frightened.

The Nutcracker quickly sprang into action. He grabbed a toy sword and led his army of tin soldiers against the mice. It was a fierce battle. The tin soldiers fought bravely. And so did the mice.

Screeeech! Marie heard a sharp whistle. The battle stopped. Everyone turned to see what the noise was. And there, at the foot of the tree, was the most curious creature Marie had ever seen.

It was a giant mouse—much bigger than any of the others. And, instead of one head, it had seven . . . each wearing a tiny golden crown. This was the Mouse King.

The Mouse King challenged the Nutcracker to a duel. What a horrible sight! The Nutcracker fought as best he could. But the ugly beast seemed to be everywhere at once. Finally, the Nutcracker fell to the ground. And the Mouse King was just about to pounce on him.

Terrified, Marie threw her slipper at the Mouse King. He was furious, and now he came after Marie. The poor girl was so frightened, she fainted. In that same instant, the Nutcracker bravely killed the Mouse King with his sword. The battle was over.

Proudly, the Nutcracker held one of the Mouse King's golden crowns above his head. As he did this, the little wooden man changed into a handsome young Prince. At once, everything else began to change, too.

The mice and the toys disappeared. Snow began to fall in great swirling gusts. And, before she knew what was happening, Marie was sailing through space with the Prince.

"Don't be frightened," he told her. "You saved my life. And now I am taking you to see the Kingdom of Sweets."

And so Marie began the most wonderful adventure of all. She and the Prince landed in a beautiful forest. Its trees were filled with thousands of tiny white candles. Lovely ripe fruit hung from all the branches.

"This is the Christmas Forest," said the Prince.

Next, they sailed together in a walnut shell

down the River of Lemonade. All along the shore were houses made of candy. The roofs were covered with sugar icing, and the chimneys were made of jelly beans.

"This is all part of the magic land ruled by the Sugar Plum Fairy," explained the Prince.

As he spoke, they came to a magnificent palace. It was made completely of spun sugar. Just then, the Sugar Plum Fairy appeared. She was delighted to see them.

"Come inside," she said. After she had heard the story of their battle with the Mouse King, she said, "We shall celebrate your victory."

Inside the palace, tables were filled with every kind of sweet. There were chocolates and nougats and bonbons of all sizes and flavors. And then, the Sugar Plum Fairy danced for them. What a wonderful dance it was. Marie and the Prince joined in. And, finally, all the sweets and bonbons got up and danced with them.

Marie wished she could stay forever. But soon it was time to leave. A lovely white sleigh appeared. It was pulled by magic reindeer. As Marie and the Prince climbed in, the reindeer flew into the sky. Marie waved good-bye to the dancing Kingdom of Sweets. And away she sailed into the snowy night.

Marie climbed higher and higher into the sky.

The snow grew thicker and thicker. Everything was white, and Marie felt so sleepy. . . .

On Christmas morning, Marie awoke. There she was in her very own bed. Christmas—the day she loved more than any other—had finally come. Quickly, Marie raced downstairs to see the tree.

And there, in his own little bed, lay the Nutcracker. He was just as she had left him—only he wasn't broken anymore. He was as good as new—just as Herr Drosselmeyer had promised. What a wonderful Christmas surprise!

The Twelve Days of Christmas

Traditional English Carol

On the first day of Christmas
My true love gave to me
A partridge in a pear tree.

On the second day of Christmas
My true love gave to me
Two turtledoves
And a partridge in a pear tree.

On the third day of Christmas
My true love gave to me
Three French hens,
Two turtledoves,
And a partridge in a pear tree.

On the fourth day of Christmas
My true love gave to me
Four calling birds,
Three French hens,
Two turtledoves,
And a partridge in a pear tree.

On the fifth day of Christmas
My true love gave to me
Five gold rings,
Four calling birds,
Three French hens,
Two turtledoves,
And a partridge in a pear tree.

On the sixth day of Christmas
My true love gave to me
Six geese a-laying,
Five gold rings,
Four calling birds,
Three French hens,
Two turtledoves,
And a partridge in a pear tree.

On the seventh day of Christmas
My true love gave to me
Seven swans a-swimming,
Six geese a-laying,
Five gold rings,
Four calling birds,
Three French hens,
Two turtledoves,
And a partridge in a pear tree.

On the eighth day of Christmas
My true love gave to me
Eight maids a-milking,
Seven swans a-swimming,
Six geese a-laying,
Five gold rings,
Four calling birds,
Three French hens,
Two turtledoves,
And a partridge in a pear tree.

On the ninth day of Christmas
My true love gave to me
Nine ladies dancing,
Eight maids a-milking,
Seven swans a-swimming,
Six geese a-laying,
Five gold rings,
Four calling birds,
Three French hens,
Two turtledoves,
And a partridge in a pear tree.

On the tenth day of Christmas
My true love gave to me
Ten lords a-leaping,

Nine ladies dancing,
Eight maids a-milking,
Seven swans a-swimming,
Six geese a-laying,
Five gold rings,
Four calling birds,
Three French hens,
Two turtledoves,
And a partridge in a pear tree.

On the eleventh day of Christmas
My true love gave to me
Eleven pipers piping,
Ten lords a-leaping,
Nine ladies dancing,
Eight maids a-milking,
Seven swans a-swimming,
Six geese a-laying,
Five gold rings,
Four calling birds,
Three French hens,
Two turtledoves,
And a partridge in a pear tree.

On the twelfth day of Christmas
My true love gave to me
Twelve drummers drumming,

Eleven pipers piping,
Ten lords a-leaping,
Nine ladies dancing,
Eight maids a-milking,
Seven swans a-swimming,
Six geese a-laying,
Five gold rings,
Four calling birds,
Three French hens,
Two turtledoves,
And a partridge in a pear tree.

Recipes

Everybody loves homemade goodies at Christmastime. Make these treats to give as gifts, to decorate your tree, or to eat with a friend.

Popcorn Balls

½ cup (120 ml) sugar
½ cup (120 ml) light corn syrup
¼ cup (60 ml) butter or margarine
8 cups (1.9 l) plain popped corn

Place the sugar, corn syrup, and margarine into a large pot. Stirring constantly, heat the ingredients over a medium-high heat. Stir the popcorn into the mixture, and heat for 3 more minutes. Make sure the popcorn is well coated. Remove from heat. Let the mixture cool slightly before you touch it.

Dip your hands in cold water. Take handfuls of the mixture and shape into 2½-inch (6-cm) balls. Place the balls on waxed paper to cool. Wrap each ball in plastic wrap or colored cellophane.

YIELD: 8 or 9 balls

NOTE: If you want to make colored popcorn balls, add a few drops of food coloring to the hot mixture before you add the popcorn.

Sugar Cookie Cutouts

1 cup (.24 l) butter or margarine, softened
3 tbsp. (44 ml) milk
1 cup (.24 l) sugar
3 cups (.72 l) flour
1 large egg
1 tsp. (5 ml) baking powder
½ tsp. (2.5 ml) salt
1 tsp. (5 ml) vanilla
cookie cutters

Preheat oven to 400°F (204°C).

In a large bowl, cream the butter and sugar together using an electric mixer. Beat in the milk, egg, and vanilla until well blended. Add the baking powder and salt. Gradually add the flour and mix well.

Wrap the dough in waxed paper and refrigerate for one hour.

Remove the dough from the refrigerator and divide into 2 balls. On a floured surface, roll the first ball into a 12-inch (30.5-cm) circle. The dough should be about ⅜ inch (.95 cm) thick.

Choose a cookie cutter and dip it in flour. Press the floured cutter firmly into the dough. If the dough gets stuck inside the cookie cutter, tap the cutter on a flat surface until the dough comes away from the cookie cutter.

Place the cutouts on a shiny, ungreased cookie sheet and bake for 6–8 minutes, until the edges are light brown. Remove cookies from the oven and transfer them to wire racks or paper towels to cool.

YIELD: Varies depending on the size of the cookie cutters.

HINT: You can decorate your cutouts with prepared frosting, sprinkles, chocolate candies, or other treats.

Chocolate Snowcaps

1¾ cups (.42 l) flour
½ cup (120 ml) sugar
½ cup (120 ml) firmly packed brown sugar
1 tsp. (5 ml) baking soda
½ tsp. (2.5 ml) salt
½ cup (120 ml) butter or margarine
½ cup (120 ml) peanut butter
2 tbsp. (30 ml) milk
1 tsp. (5 ml) vanilla
1 large egg
extra sugar (for rolling)
48 chocolate Kisses

Preheat oven to 375°F (190°C).

In a small bowl, combine the flour, baking soda, and salt. Set aside.

In a large bowl combine the sugar, brown sugar, milk, butter, vanilla, and egg. Beat until creamy. Add the peanut butter and mix well. Gradually combine the flour mixture until a stiff dough forms.

Shape dough into 1-inch (2.5-cm) balls. Roll the balls in the extra sugar. Place balls 2 inches

(5 cm) apart on an ungreased cookie sheet.

Bake for 10–12 minutes, or until golden brown. Remove cookie sheet from oven. Immediately place a chocolate Kiss in the center of each cookie, pressing down firmly. Transfer cookies to a wire rack.

YIELD: 48 cookies

Gingerbread Kids

¼ cup (60 ml) butter or margarine
½ cup (120 ml) sugar
½ cup (120 ml) molasses
3½ cups (.84 l) flour
1 tsp. (5 ml) baking soda
½ tsp. (2.5 ml) cinnamon
1 tsp. (5 ml) ginger
½ tsp. (2.5 ml) salt
¼ cup (60 ml) water
icing and sprinkles

Preheat oven to 350°F (177°C).

In a large bowl, beat butter and sugar until fluffy. Add molasses and beat well.

Gradually add the flour and beat well. Add baking soda, cinnamon, ginger, salt, and water. Mix well.

Grease a baking sheet with margarine or cooking spray. Roll the dough out on a floured surface until it is ¼"-½" (.63-1.3 cm) thick. Use a "gingerbread kid" cookie cutter to make shapes (or use any cookie cutter you like). Place the cutouts on a greased baking sheet and bake for 8 minutes or until cookies are set. Transfer cutouts to a wire rack to cool.

Decorate your gingerbread kids with icing, sprinkles, or small candies.

YIELD: About 3½ dozen gingerbread kids

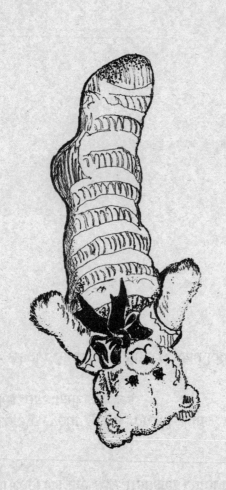